PIANO.

STRINGS

PIANO

VIOLINS

So off went the old man out into the garden, pretending to be a lion. But no matter how grand he tried to look, the chickens were not impressed. They stood about on their dainty legs, idly pecking at some corn.

Why, all you have to do is look, and you can see that he is not a lion at all, just a nice old man with a shaggy beard and twinkling eyes.

"Go away, old man. Don't disturb us," the chickens cackled.

The donkey seemed a bit curious, though. He came trotting up to see what the fuss was about.

By now the sun was rising, but the old man felt fed up and a bit sleepy. He kicked off his slippers, lay down on top of a little hill and soon began to snore.

Then something mysterious happened. Very slowly and very quietly the hill began to move. It swayed and it lumbered along.

"Who's sitting on my back?" an ancient voice boomed.

It was the giant tortoise. He was going to visit his old friend the elephant.

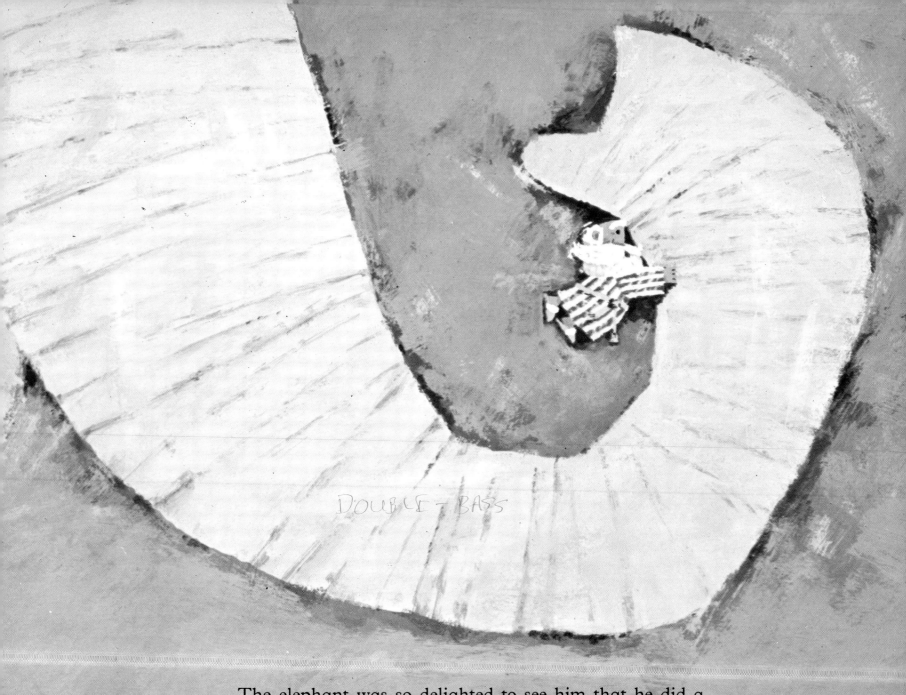

The elephant was so delighted to see him that he did a little dance. Around and around he waltzed with his great big cushioned feet.

Suddenly the old man sat up. "No, no. That's much too clumsy," he said. "Can't you skip, lightly and brightly? Please lift me off this hill, so I can show you how."

Gently the elephant lifted him down with his trunk, and away the old man skipped.

Then something came bounding up to meet him. It looked like a large, hopping pocket with a huge tail on one end.

"What?" it exclaimed. "Haven't you got a tail? Only pockets and legs? You'll never pass for a proper kangaroo!"

Soon he came to the lake. He peered down through the rippling surface until his nose got wet. And there, in the deep, clear water, were hundreds of gleaming fish.

"Hey! Fish! Fishy! Come here! Come here!"

"No," they said. "We won't come unless you call us by our right names."

Swish! They flicked their tails and darted away, leaving lots of little bubbles floating upwards.

"Stop, you! You can't catch fish here," somebody screeched.

"What? I wasn't catching them. I was only watching them."

"Hmph! You looked to me as though you were trying to catch them."

"Oh, I did, did I? And just what do you know about it, pray tell? You're nothing but a stubborn old mule!"

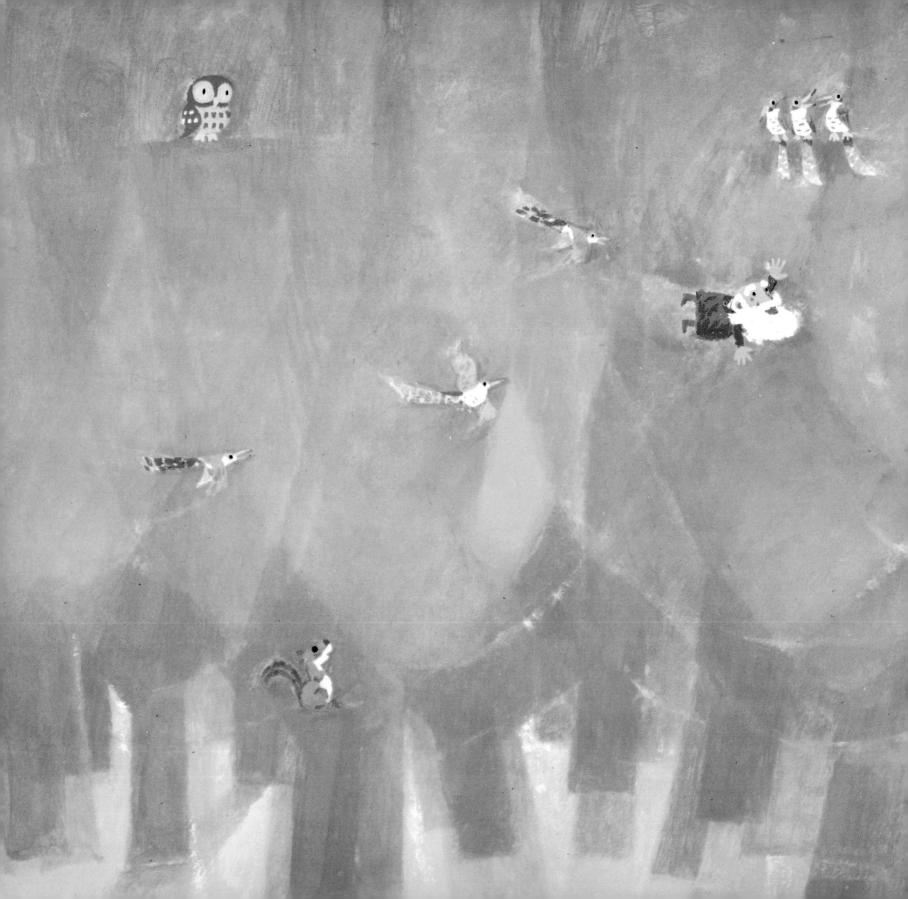

The old man needed something to calm his ruffled feelings, and what could be better than a stroll in the forest?

One, two, three trees. Four trees, six trees, twenty trees. But no matter how many tall, shady trees he counted, he never quite reached the place where the cuckoos sang. They were too clever. They always stayed a little bit ahead of him.

The old man began to feel much better.

He thought he would try some magic, so he took his silver flute out of his pocket and flung it up towards the sun. Suddenly it sprouted wings and flew away into the air singing sweetly as it went. The little birds trilled and warbled in amazement.

What sort of a magician could he be?

Then he stopped by a house where a young man was practising the piano.

"You'll have to do better than that," the old man shouted, sticking his fingers in his ears. "But you're only a beginner, and you've a long way to go. You still can't keep up with the flute that soars in the sky. Work hard so that you can."

"I will," the young man answered, and went on playing harder than ever.

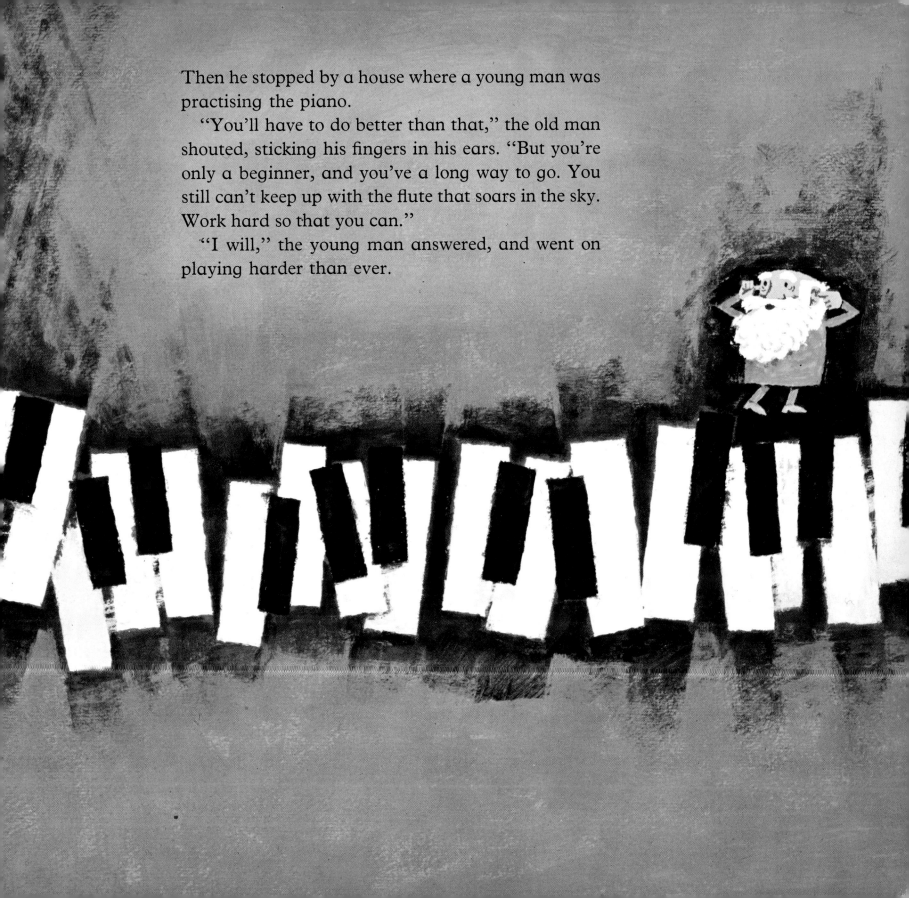

As he wandered on, the old man thought back. He remembered times long past. He remembered being the same age as the young man playing the piano, only much better-looking, of course. He thought of times before that, all the way back to his childhood and to when he was a baby. His mother used to sing him songs. What lovely songs they were.

Then he called to mind a fairy-tale. A tale about a princess who was always dressed in white. A princess with a slender neck and elegant head, wearing a silver crown.

The old man tugged at his moustache and looked thoughtful.

"Ah," he whispered to himself. "A princess like a swan."

Now here you will see a very distinguished gentleman. If you look closely, you will discover that he is none other than our old friend with the shaggy beard. But now his beard is neatly combed and trimmed, for tonight the old man wants to look smart.

Just who is he really? Perhaps you have already guessed. He is a famous French composer, and his name is Camille Saint-Saëns.

He and all the animals are off to a concert, so now they have come to say good-bye.